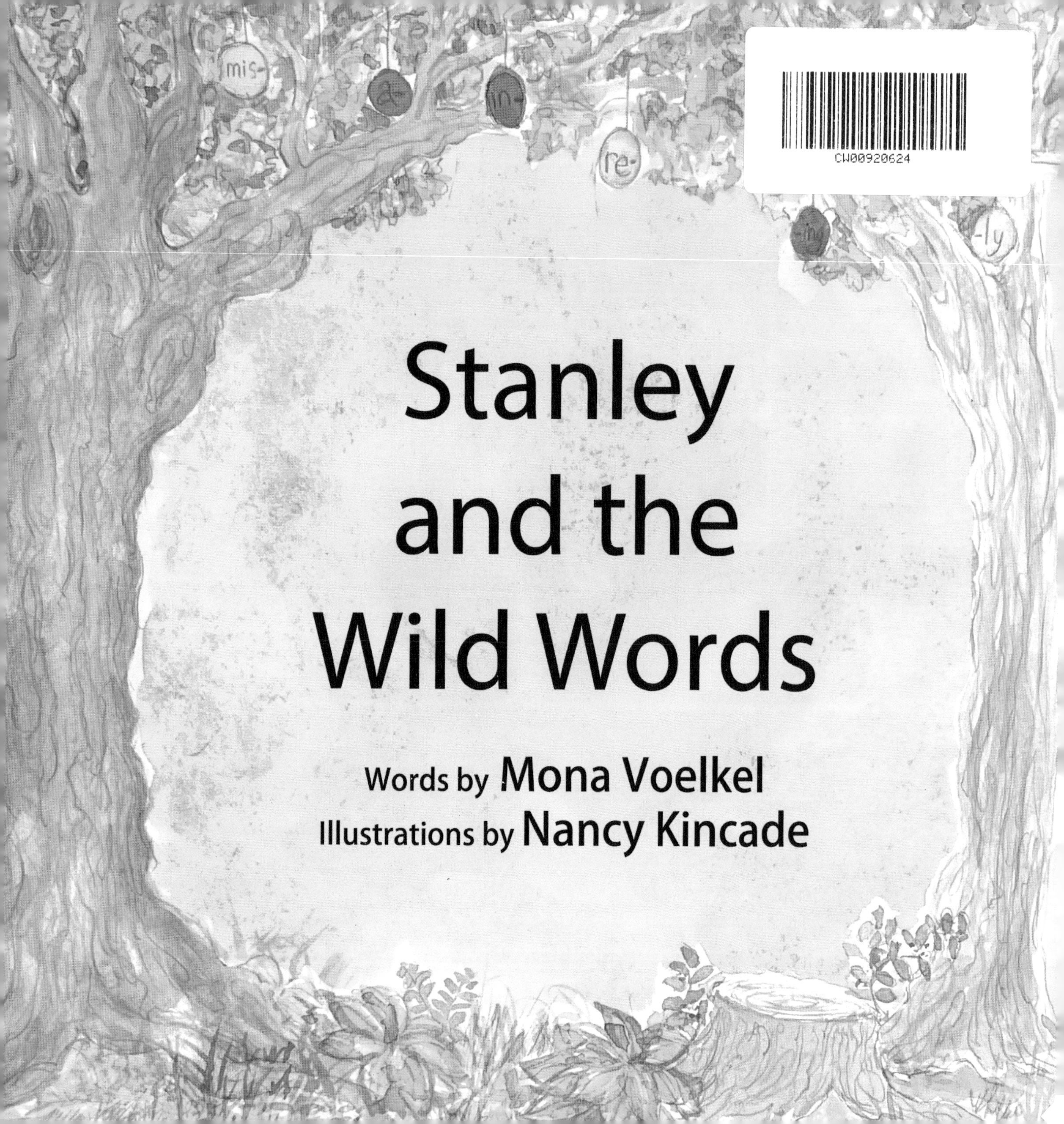

Stanley and the Wild Words

Words by Mona Voelkel
Illustrations by Nancy Kincade

For Kevin Martin.

-M.V.

For “The Fam.”

-N.K.

For Sal J. Miele, Matthew C. Curran,
and the staff and students of Kensico School.

I'm winning this writing contest, Stanley thought. He'd worked night and day so everyone could hear his story.

Time for Science
Friday
Specials
Chorus
Phys ED
MYSTERY
Reader
Coming
Soon
ACTIVITIES
Science Fair
Jody
Seth
Week of
Certificate

Stanley didn't win.

"All I ever hear is *spelling*, *spelling*, *spelling*."

"I'm never writing again."

Stanley crumpled up his story. He kicked the trash can so hard a book fell off his bookshelf and hit him on the head.

Chaos

He woke up in the Forest of Wild Words. CHAOS and RUMPUS nearly knocked him down. Stanley sidestepped to avoid BELLIGERENT then squeezed between slumbering SLOTH and curious QUESTION.

"Hi, I'm Pete. What's this about you never writing again?"
"I'm not writing because I can't spell."

“Spelling was hard for me, too,” Pete said,
“until I started asking questions about words.”

"Well I have a question. Why doesn't spelling make sense?"

"Let's see," said Pete. "What's the wildest word you know?"

"ENORMOUS."

"Do you know what it means?" asked Pete.

"Very big."

"Excellent."

Pete put a book on Stanley's lap.
Stanley read the title. "Etymology?"
Pete smiled. "In this book we can find a word's history.
The history gives clues about meaning and spelling."

“ENORMOUS comes from Latin,” explained Pete.
“In Latin, *norma* means ‘rule.’
The word ENORMOUS still carries a sense of ‘rule.’”

"But ENORMOUS doesn't mean rule."

"See this E-?" Pete said.

"It adds the idea of 'out of' to our base, NORM."

Stanley's face brightened. "So, something ENORMOUS is something outside the rule? My dragon's ENORMOUS teeth were bigger than NORMAL?"

"Yes," Pete said as he swung. "Now you're getting it."
"Pete," beamed Stanley, "this is an ENORMOUS discovery."

a-
-es
-ly
-ed
dis-
im-
ex-
-ion
-able
in-
un-
re-
mis-
pre-
e-
-er
-s
The Suffix Tree
-ing
-ent
-or
The Prefix Tree
a
m
o
u
s

Pete laughed. “It’s time to meet the family.
NORM family, meet Stanley.”

“ENORMOUS has so many relatives!” exclaimed Stanley.

Pete picked up a stick.
"And now, Stanley, instead of sounding out our word, let's think about how it's built."

"Let's spell out each part."

"Next, we'll connect sounds to letters in the base. How many sounds do you hear and feel when you say NORM?"

“Three,” said Stanley.
Then Stanley spelled out the whole word:
“E—N-OR-M—OUS.
Pete, spelling does make sense!”

Pete nodded, “Questions about words,
like stories shared with friends,
will lead you to magical places.”

In a flash, Stanley was back in his room.

There, on his desk, was Pete's hat, a pencil, and a book.
He put on the hat, took his story out of the trash,
and picked out a word to explore.
Stanley had stories waiting to be shared.

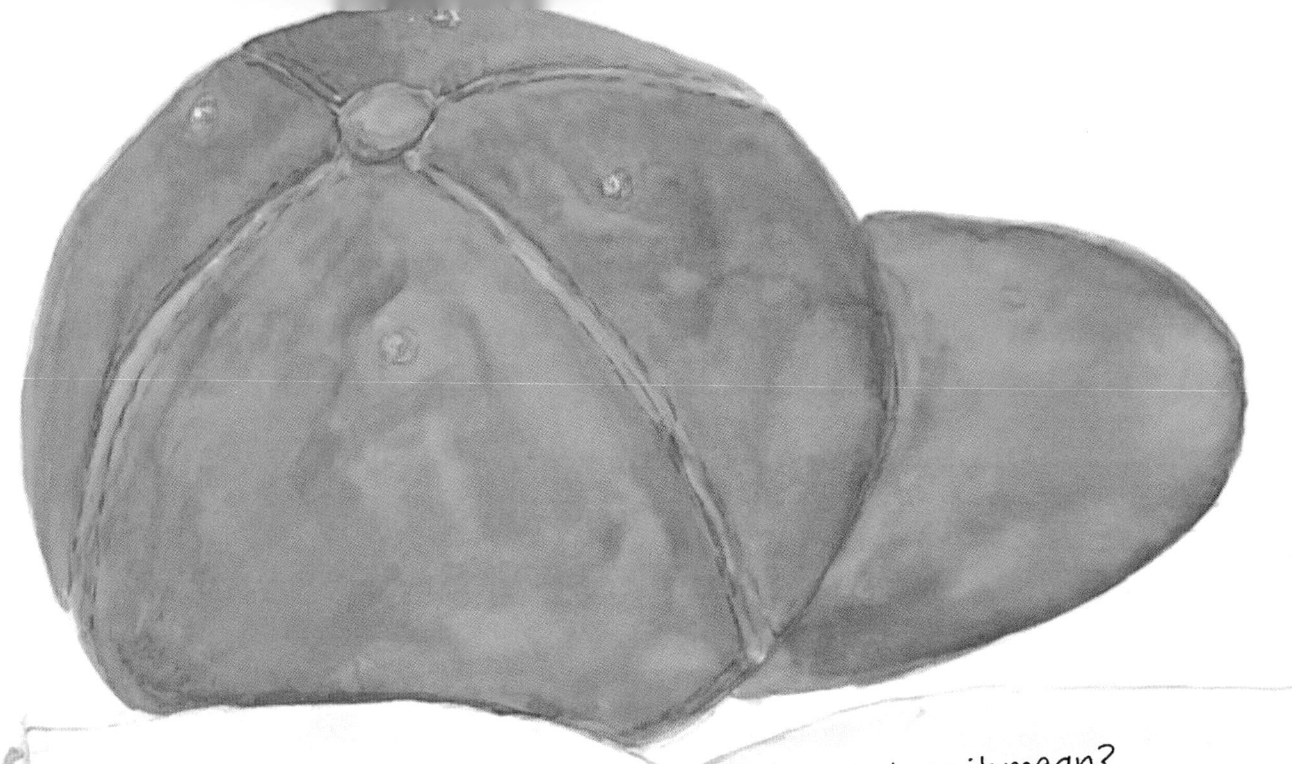

Dear Stanley,

I hope you continue your **quest** to understand spelling.

Just start with an interesting word.

Here are some **quest**ions to guide your word investigations:

1. What does it mean?
2. Who are its relatives?
3. How is it built?
4. How many sounds do you hear and feel?

Happy **quest**ing,

Pete

P.S. My only re**quest** is you share what you've learned with others.

My deepest thanks to Marye Elmlinger, Nancy and John Kincade, Monica Durkan, Cathy Cahill, William Voelkel, Ada Parker, Claire Mendick, Kimberly Hedzik, Dianne Koebler-Pede, Mark McGrath, Maggie Dixon, Cheryl Wolf, Jude Westerfield, Suzanne Ross, Ryan Pellak, Gail Venable, Naomi Suster, and the SWI community.

Love and thanks to my cherished family: Raymond, Kevin, Meredith, Kieran Martin, Cormac McKinney, Brian and Enya. Marty, you are always in our hearts.

Edited by Marye Elmlinger

Thanks to Dr. Peter Bowers for sharing the principles of Structured Word Inquiry that inspired this book.Visit his website to learn more at https://www.wordworkskingston.com.
Thanks to Doug Harper for the "Online Etymological Dictionary."
Visit his resource at https://www.etymonline.com.

Names: Voelkel, Mona, author. | Kincade, Nancy, illustrator.
Title: Stanley and the wild words / by Mona Voelkel and illustrated by Nancy Kincade.
Publisher: Dobbs Ferry, NY: Arigna Press, 2022. | Summary: Stanley is tired of his terrible spelling. Journey with Stanley to the forest of Wild Words and learn a secret about spelling!
Identifiers: LCCN: 2022901341 |
ISBN: 978-1-7376955-0-9 (paperback) | 978-1-7376955-1-6 (epub) / 978-1-7376955-2-3 (hardback)

Subjects: LCSH English language--Juvenile fiction. | Language and languages--Orthography and spelling--Juvenile fiction. | Friendship--Fiction. | BISAC JUVENILE FICTION / General | JUVENILE FICTION / Concepts / Words
Classification: LCC PZ7.1.V645 Sta 2022 | DDC [E]—dc23

Thie text of this book is set in Lora.
The illustrations were rendered in pencil and watercolor.

About the Author:

Mona Voelkel is an award-winning reading specialist with a passion for picture books. When she and her students discovered that spelling really does make sense, they were empowered beyond words.

Visit www.monavoelkel.com, where you can investigate words from the story, sign up for a newsletter, or contact her for a school visit.

Contact is from the Latin contactus, "touching."

con + tact --> contact
"together" "touch"

About the Illustrator:

Nancy Kincade won a Christopher Award for *Even If I Did Something Awful*, one of several books she illustrated for Atheneum Books.

After a very enjoyable career in art education, she is delighted to be illustrating once again. Her most recent books include *A God of Purpose: Fareena's Friendship* and *A God of Redemption: Hannah's Heartache*.

Nancy can be contacted at mckinne4j@gmail.com.

Printed in Great Britain
by Amazon